LOOK AND FIND®

FRIENDS & FAVORITES

Illustrated by
the Disney Storybook Artists and Art Mawhinney

Published by Louis Weber, C.E.O., Publications International, Ltd.
7373 North Cicero Avenue, Lincolnwood, Illinois 60712
Ground Floor, 59 Gloucester Place, London W1U 8JJ

Customer Service: 1-800-595-8484 or customer_service@pilbooks.com

www.pilbooks.com

Manufactured in China.

p i kids is a registered trademark of Publications International, Ltd.
Look and Find is a registered trademark of Publications International, Ltd.,
in the United States and in Canada.

8 7 6 5 4 3 2 1

ISBN-13: 978-1-4127-1053-4
ISBN-10: 1-4127-1053-7

publications international, ltd.

There are so many toys and games inside Al's Toy Barn! Buzz, Rex, and Hamm have been searching for Woody among the shelves, but the only luck they've had has been finding a guidebook to defeating the evil Emperor Zurg for the Buzz Lightyear video game!

Look through the toys to find Buzz, Rex, Hamm, and these crazy characters they have met here.

Dirk Soldier

Rex

Buzz

Speedy Racer

Hamm

Rhonda Ragdoll

Evil Emperor Zurg

This is the new Laugh Floor, and the monsters are going about things a little differently. They are having lots of fun, but it is still hard work. Not everyone is a comedian. Lend a hand by finding these funny things for the monsters to use.

Squirting flower

Can of nuts

Whoopee cushion

Pie for throwing

Banana peel

Pair of funny glasses

Clown nose

Trick arrow

Today is Nemo's first day of school. He and his father Marlin meet the teacher, Mr. Ray. Oh no, Nemo has wandered off with some of his classmates! Can you locate Nemo, his new school chums, their parents, and Mr. Ray in all this hustle and bustle?

Nemo

Pearl

Ted

Phil

Sheldon

Bob

Tad

Mr. Ray

It's over to the Island of Nomanisan for some heart-pounding action! The Incredibles have their hands full, battling Syndrome and his team of guards. Now take a quick break from the combat to search the volcanic island for these tropical fruits.

A comely kumquat

A magnificent mango

A beautiful banana

A palatable papaya

A gorgeous guava

A passionate passion fruit

A fuzzy kiwi

Welcome to Flo's V8 Cafe. There are always plenty of treats to keep your engine a-purring and your tires a-turning. See if you can find these motor-watering morsels.

Ice Cold Coolant

Mouthwatering Motor Oil

Transmission fluid

Wiper fluid

Anti-Freeze Frosty

Car wax

Linguini opens the door to the restaurant's walk-in refrigerator to find a surprise — rats! Emile has led the entire colony to Gusteau's, and now they are stealing all the food they can get their paws on. Look through the shelves of food to find these rats.

WALL•E's job is to clean up Earth. As he makes cubes of garbage and stacks them high, look for these pieces of trash.

Newspaper

Rubber duck

Refrigerator

Bottle

Fire extinguisher

Shopping cart

Boot

Up, up, and away! Carl and Russell are going for a mile-high adventure to South America—in Carl's house! Look down onto the city and spot these people going about their business on the ground below.

Hot dog vendor

Little girl in apartment

Secretary

Street musician

Newspaper vendor

Window washer

Andy's toys did not find Woody inside Al's Toy Barn, but they did find a clue leading them to Woody's whereabouts. Go back to the Toy Barn and find these things that could help them with their detective work:

A Magnifying Glass
A Fingerprint Kit
A Box of Disguises
A Telescope
A Bow Tie Camera
A Secret-Spy Decoder Ring

Laughter is the best energy! Go back to the Laugh Floor to find these silly monsters who make kids laugh:

A monster in a bucket
A shadow-puppet monster
A trick-photographer monster
A ventriloquist monster
An upside-down monster
A tutu-wearing monster
A tap-dancing monster
A juggling monster

Swim on back to the reef to find these school-related things:

Stones in the shape of a math problem
Jar of squid ink
Seaweed macrame
Algae map of Australia

Now you're off to the Island of Nomanisan, this time to find these different Omnidroids:

X1	X5
X2	X6
X3	X7
X4	X8

Pull back into Flo's V8 Cafe to find as many of these tasty treats as you can:

5 more cans of oil
10 cans of lube
10 cans of wax
8 boxes of car soap
3 cans of grease
4 boxes of filters

Step back into the walk-in refrigerator at Gusteau's to look for these fine foods:

Caviar

Cheese wheel

Fine chocolates

Lobster

Rib eye steaks

Grapes

WALL•E loves to collect the most interesting bits of junk. But he has his own idea of what's valuable. Go back to the work site and find these things that WALL•E didn't think were worth keeping:

Gold Coin

Vase

Diamond ring

Gold watch

Money

Jeweled necklace

Soar back over the city and see if you can find these modes of transportation: